Otter B
HELPFUL

WRITTEN BY
Pamela Kennedy & Anne Kennedy Brady

ILLUSTRATED BY
Aaron Zenz

Tyndale House Publishers
Carol Stream, Illinois

FOCUS ON THE FAMILY®

Otter B: Helpful
© 2019 Pamela Kennedy and Anne Kennedy Brady. All rights reserved.
Illustrations © 2019 Focus on the Family

A Focus on the Family book published by Tyndale House Publishers, Inc.,
Carol Stream, Illinois 60188

Focus on the Family and the accompanying logo and design are federally
registered trademarks of Focus on the Family, 8605 Explorer Drive,
Colorado Springs, CO 80920.

TYNDALE and Tyndale's quill logo are registered trademarks of Tyndale
House Publishers, Inc.

All Scripture quotations, unless otherwise indicated, are taken from the *Holy
Bible, New International Reader's Version*,® NIrV.® Copyright © 1995,
1996, 1998, 2014 by Biblica, Inc.® Used by permission of Zondervan. All
rights reserved worldwide. (*www.zondervan.com*) The "NIrV" and "New
International Reader's Version" are trademarks registered in the United
States Patent and Trademark Office by Biblica, Inc. ®

Cover design by Josh Lewis
Cover illustration by Aaron Zenz

Book Design by Josh Lewis
Text set in Source Sans and Prater Sans Pro.

For manufacturing information regarding this product, please call
1-800-323-9400.

For information about special discounts for bulk purchases, please contact
Tyndale House Publishers at csresponse@tyndale.com, or call 1-800-323-9400.

Library of Congress Cataloging-in-Publication Data can be found at
www.loc.gov.

ISBN 978-1-58997-047-2

Printed in China

28   27   26   25   24   23   22
8   7   6   5   4   3   2

Otter B watched raindrops make
little rivers down the windows.
Rain pitter-pattered in puddles outside.
He loved sliding and splashing in the
water, but today the weather was cold.
He decided to play indoors instead.

Otter B dumped out his blocks and built a
pretend forest with tall trees and a winding creek.

Then he drew pictures of all his friends.

After that, he made a tent with a blanket and
piled up a bunch of pillows, like a nest.
He crawled inside and read books to
his stuffed animals.

"Goodness!" said Mama.
"Grammy and Papa are coming for lunch, and this place is a mess!"

Otter B peeked out from his tent. Books and blocks, paper and crayons, blankets and stuffed animals covered the floor. He looked up at Mama with big eyes.

"I can help put your books away," she offered.

Otter B scrambled over to his block forest.

"I'll cut down my forest and stack the blocks back in the bin. Let's make a game!"

Mama and Otter B raced to see who could finish first.
Then they lined up the stuffed animals
from tallest to smallest.

They folded the blanket together, and Otter B put it back on the chair.

Then they had a pillow fight.

"**That was fun!**" Otter B giggled.
"**Thanks for helping me!**"

Mama looked at the clock.
"**Oh! I need to fix lunch.**"

"**Maybe I can help you now!**"
Otter B suggested.

Mama gave Otter B four forks and four napkins.
He placed a napkin next to everyone's plate
and then put a fork on top of each napkin.

"What's next?" he asked.

Mama let Otter B stand on a stool and wash tiny tomatoes and baby carrots for a salad while she tore lettuce leaves into small pieces. They mixed all the vegetables together in a big bowl. Then Otter B poured some of his favorite fishy crackers in a basket.

"I know another way I can help!" said Otter B.

He tore a sheet of paper into four pieces.
He colored one pink, one blue, one green, and one brown.
Then he put one on each plate.

Ding Dong! The doorbell rang. Grammy and Papa had arrived!

"Come, see the table!" said Otter B as Mama invited them in. As he bounded around the table, Otter B pointed to the colored papers he'd made.

"Papa, you sit at the brown place because that is the color of your favorite hat!" he said.

"Grammy, your place is pink because that's your favorite color! Mama, yours is green because you grow tasty things in the garden. And my place is blue, because water is blue and I love it!"

They all sat down at their special places and started eating.

"This salad is delicious!" said Grammy.

As Papa crunched into a cracker, he looked around and said,
**"The room is so neat and tidy! You two have
been working hard this morning."**

Mama winked at Otter B.
**"Work is fun when you have
a helper! Right, Otter B?"**

Otter B nodded.
His mouth was full of crackers!

There's always lots of work to do in every family.
God says that helping out is best.

It's how you Otter Be!

*Let us not become
tired of doing good.*
Galatians 6:9